MARTHA SPEAKS®

Toy Trouble

MARTHA HABLA

Problemas con un juguete

Written by Karen Barss | Escrito por Karen Barss

Translated by Carlos E. Calvo | Traducido al español por Carlos E. Calvo

Based on the characters created by Susan Meddaugh
Basado en los personajes creados por Susan Meddaugh

HOUGHTON MIFFLIN HARCOURT
Boston · New York

For information about permission to reproduce selections from this book, write to
Permissions, Houghton Mifflin Harcourt Publishing Company, 215 Park Avenue South,
New York, New York 10003.

ISBN: 978-0-544-50390-8 paper-over-board
ISBN: 978-0-544-50389-2 paperback

www.hmhco.com
www.marthathetalkingdog.com

Manufactured in China
SCP 10 9 8 7 6 5 4 3 2 1
4500541420

AGES	GRADES	GUIDED READING LEVEL	READING RECOVERY LEVEL	LEXILE® LEVEL	SPANISH LEXILE® LEVEL
5 – 7	K – 2	J	17	320L	270L

T.D. has a surprise for Martha and Skits.
"It's a dog toy. Watch!" he says.

T.D. tiene una sorpresa para Martha y Skits.
—Es un juguete para perros. ¡Miren! —les dice.

What's that?

¿Qué es eso?

T.D. puts his fingers into the toy squirrel's front feet.
"Now I pull," he explains, "and let go!"

T.D. pone los dedos dentro de las patas delanteras de la ardilla de juguete.
—Ahora jalo —explica—, ¡y la lanzo!

The toy flies into the air.
It makes a funny noise.
Chitter-chitter-chitter!
Martha and Skits run after the toy.

El juguete vuela por el aire.
Hace un ruido gracioso.
¡Chiti-chiti-chiti!
Martha y Skits corren detrás del juguete.

"Skits! Give it!" Martha yells.
Skits growls.
He shakes his head.
"Skits is hogging the toy!" Martha whines.

My turn!
¡Es mi turno!

—¡Skits, dámelo! —grita Martha.
Skits gruñe. Niega con la cabeza.
—¡Skits no me quiere dar el juguete! —se queja Martha.

Helen frowns.
"You have to share."
Helen frunce el ceño.
—Tienen que compartir.

"T.D. wanted us both to
have fun," Martha says.
Skits drops the toy.
Martha grins and grabs it.

—T.D. quería que ambos nos
divirtiéramos —le dice Martha.
Skits suelta el juguete.
Martha sonríe y lo agarra.

"Ha-ha! All mine," she says.

—¡Ja, ja! Ahora es mío —dice.

Skits barks. *Woof, woof!*
Martha and Skits tug on the toy.

Skits ladra. —*¡Guau, guau!*
Martha y Skits tironean del juguete.

Helen grabs the toy and walks into
the house.
The dogs follow her.
"Why did you take it away?" Martha asks.

Helen les saca el juguete y entra en la casa.
Los perros la siguen.
—¿Por qué nos lo sacas? —pregunta Martha.

"It will stay inside," Helen replies,
"until you learn to play nice."
"That could take forever!" Martha exclaims.

—Se quedará adentro —responde Helen—
hasta que aprendan a jugar como
corresponde.
—¡Para eso pasará mucho tiempo! —exclama
Martha.

"Come with me," Helen says.
She plays a video on TV.
It is a video about sharing.

—Vengan conmigo —les dice Helen.
Les pone un DVD en la tele.
Es un video que trata de compartir.

Two puppets both want a ball.

Dos títeres quieren una pelota.

A clown sings,
"When there is more than one,
playing is more fun when you share . . ."

Un payaso canta,
"Cuando hay más de uno,
es más divertido jugar compartiendo..."

"What do you say now?" Helen asks.
Martha turns to Skits.
"Let's call a truce," Martha says.
"No more fighting."

—¿Qué dicen ahora? —pregunta Helen.
Martha mira a Skits.
—Hagamos una tregua —dice Martha—.
Basta de peleas.

But Martha does not want to share.
She wants to trade toys for the squirrel.
Woof, says Skits, shaking his head.
He does not want Martha's toys.

Pero Martha no quiere compartir.
Ella quiere canjear juguetes por la ardilla.
—*Guau* —dice Skits, negando con la
cabeza.
Él no quiere los juguetes de Martha.

Martha decides to play a trick on Skits.
She points behind Skits with her nose.
"What if I give you *that*?"

Martha decide engañar a Skits.
Con el hocico, señala
detrás de Skits.
—¿Qué tal si te doy *eso*?

When Skits turns away to look,
Martha grabs the squirrel.
Skits chases her, barking.
Woof! Woof!

Cuando Skits se da vuelta para mirar,
Martha agarra la ardilla.
Skits la persigue ladrando.
¡Guau! ¡Guau!

"I told you to share!" Helen says.
Martha laughs. "We *are* sharing."
"How?" Helen asks.

—Les dije que compartan —exclama Helen.
Martha se ríe.
—*Sí*, estamos compartiendo.
—¿De qué manera? —pregunta Helen.

"I made up a new game," says Martha.
"I call it Steal the Squirrel."

Inventé un nuevo juego —dice Martha—.
Se llama "Roba la ardilla".

Martha runs outside.
Skits runs after her.
He grabs the toy and tugs.
Chitter-chitter-chitter.

Martha sale corriendo.
Skits corre detrás de ella.
Él agarra el juguete y tironea.
¡Chiti-chiti-chiti!

"But you are tugging, not sharing,"
Helen says.
"This is how dogs play," Martha explains.

Maybe it *is* fun!
Quizás sí sea
divertido.

Pero están tironeando;
no están compartiendo
—dice Helen.
—Así jugamos los perros
—explica Martha.

"There is still one problem," Helen says.
"I want to play, too!"
"That's the best idea I've heard all day!" Martha says.

—Todavía hay un problema —dice Helen.
¡Yo también quiero jugar!
—Es la mejor idea que he escuchado en todo el día! —dice Martha.

Based on the events in the story, match the picture with the word.

Según los sucesos del cuento, une cada dibujo con la palabra correspondiente.

Play
Jugar

Fight
Pelear

Hug
Abrazar

Trade
Canjear

Don't miss these
MARTHA SPEAKS
adventures:

No te pierdas estas aventuras de
MARTHA HABLA:

Fireworks for All
Fuegos artificiales para todos

Martha Camps Out
Martha va de Campamento

Martha hornea un pastel
Martha Bakes a Cake

¡Juega al sófbol!
Play Ball!

Perritos en invierno
A Winter's Tail

Conoce a Martha
Meet Martha